MEM FOX

Sleepy Bears

illustrated by KERRY ARGENT

VOYAGER BOOKS · HARCOURT, INC.

San Diego   New York   London

For Eamon, Allyn, and Dave
—M. F.

For Jasmine
—K. A.

www.HarcourtBooks.com

First copublished in Australia in 1999 by Pan Macmillan Australia Pty Ltd.
and Publishing Design Studio Pty. Ltd., Australia
First U.S. edition 1999
First Voyager Books edition 2002
Voyager Books is a trademark of Harcourt, Inc., registered in the
United States of America and/or other jurisdictions.

The Library of Congress has cataloged the hardcover edition as follows:
Fox, Mem, 1946–
Sleepy bears/Mem Fox; illustrated by Kerry Argent.
p. cm.
Summary: When winter comes, six sleepy bears are rhymed to sleep by Mother Bear.
[1. Bears—Fiction. 2. Bedtime—Fiction. 3. Sleep—Fiction. 4. Mother and child—Fiction.
5. Stories in rhyme.] I. Argent, Kerry, 1960– ill. II. Title.
PZ8.3.F8245S1 1999
[E]—dc21 98-42640
ISBN 0-15-202016-0
ISBN 0-15-216542-8 pb

H G F E D C B

The illustrations in this book were done in gouache,
watercolor, and colored pencil on illustration board.
The display type was set in Ribbon.
The text type was set in Kennerley Bold.
Printed and bound by Tien Wah Press, Singapore
Production supervision by Sandra Grebenar and Wendi Taylor
Designed by Judythe Sieck

The days were growing darker and colder.
Mother Bear shivered and called to her children.

"Come in, come in,
my beautiful bears!
Winter is here and
in winter we sleep."

"Bedtime already?" cried the bears
    as they tumbled inside.
"Oh yes," said Mother Bear.
"But there's plenty of time
    For your own special rhyme,
    If you climb into bed and snuggle in tight,
    Without any fuss and without any fight."

So the little bears jumped
into the soft feather bed
and pulled up the covers
as fast as they could.

Baxter Bear was the sleepiest.
He yawned a **BIG** yawn.

Mother Bear kissed his sleepy head and said,

"Sleep, my darling pirate,
Let your dreams come true.
Battle other pirate ships
With your fearsome crew.
Raise the skull and crossbones,
Breathe the salty air,
Find your treasure, count your gold,
And sleep without a care!"

And Baxter Bear fell *faaaast* asleep.

Then Mother Bear said, "Now who's the sleepiest? Who will be next?"

Bella Bear yawned a **BIG** yawn.

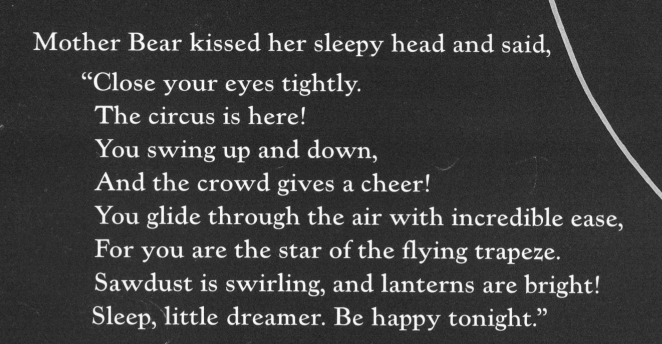

Mother Bear kissed her sleepy head and said,
"Close your eyes tightly.
The circus is here!
You swing up and down,
And the crowd gives a cheer!
You glide through the air with incredible ease,
For you are the star of the flying trapeze.
Sawdust is swirling, and lanterns are bright!
Sleep, little dreamer. Be happy tonight."

And Bella Bear fell *faaaast* asleep.

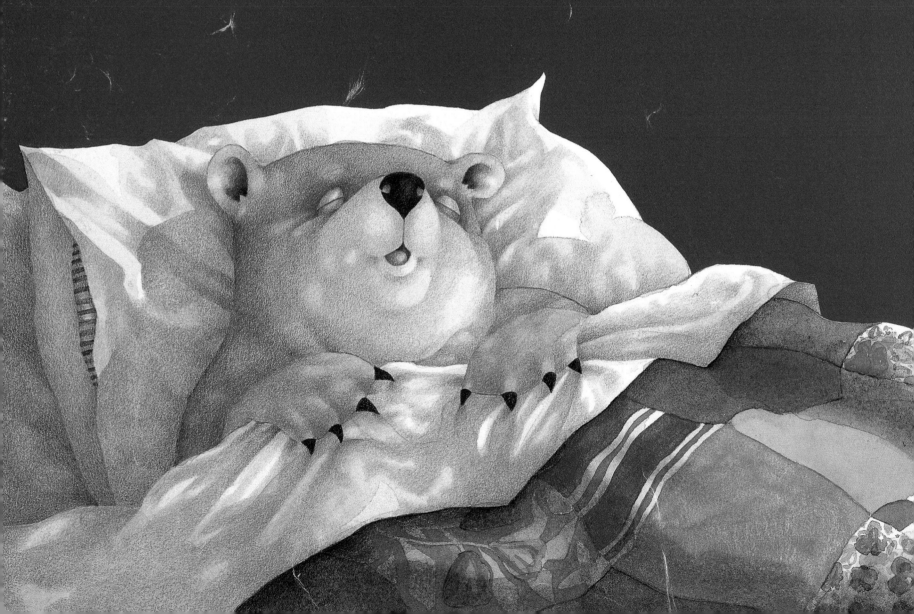

Then Mother Bear said, "Now who's the sleepiest? Who will be next?"

Winifred Bear yawned a BIG yawn.

Mother Bear kissed her sleepy head and said,

"Dare, dare, double dare!
  Where is the tiger asleep in his lair?
  You creep through the jungle
  While old chimpanzees
  Chatter and roar from the tops of the trees.
  A tiger, a tiger! You're on to his trail!
  A tiger, a tiger! Grab hold of his tail!
  Dream of adventure, dream without care,
  And sleep very soundly, my brave little bear."

And Winifred Bear fell *faaaast* asleep.

Then Mother Bear said, "Now who's the sleepiest? Who will be next?"

Tosca Bear yawned a BIG yawn.

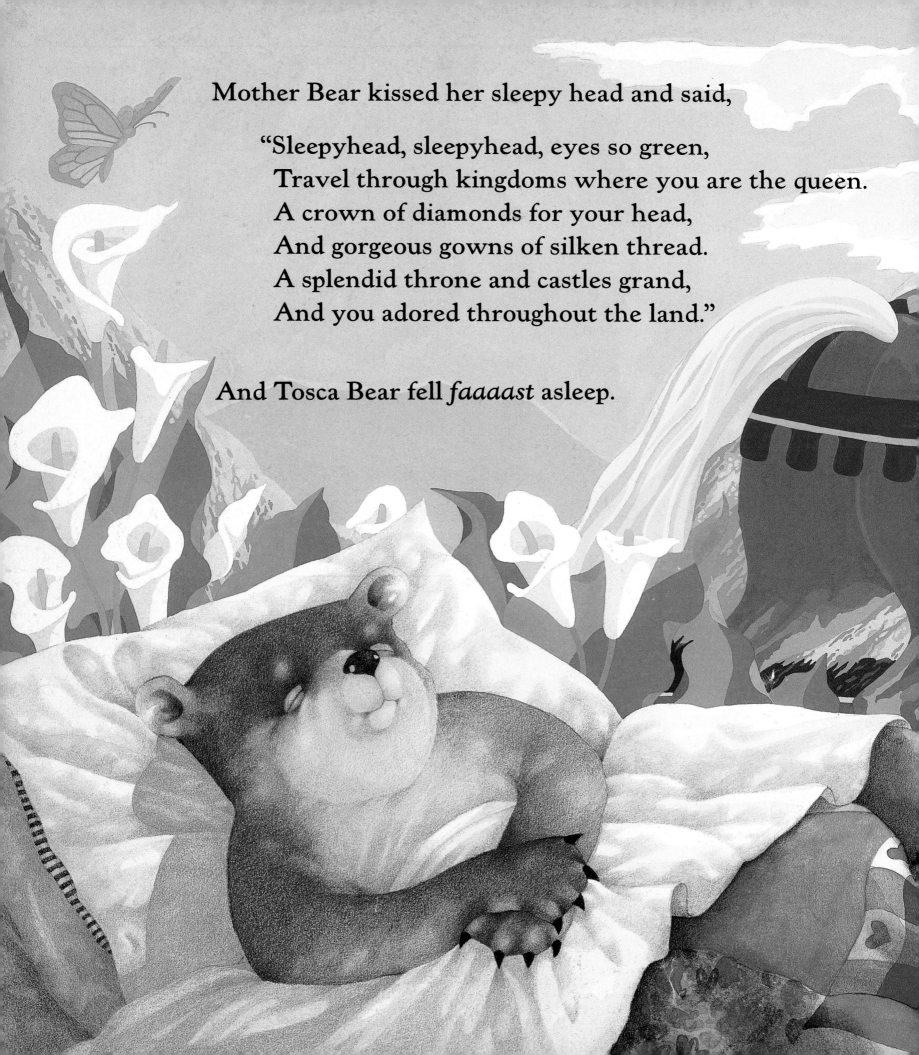

Mother Bear kissed her sleepy head and said,

"Sleepyhead, sleepyhead, eyes so green,
Travel through kingdoms where you are the queen.
A crown of diamonds for your head,
And gorgeous gowns of silken thread.
A splendid throne and castles grand,
And you adored throughout the land."

And Tosca Bear fell *faaaast* asleep.

Then Mother Bear said, "Now who's the sleepiest? Who will be next?"

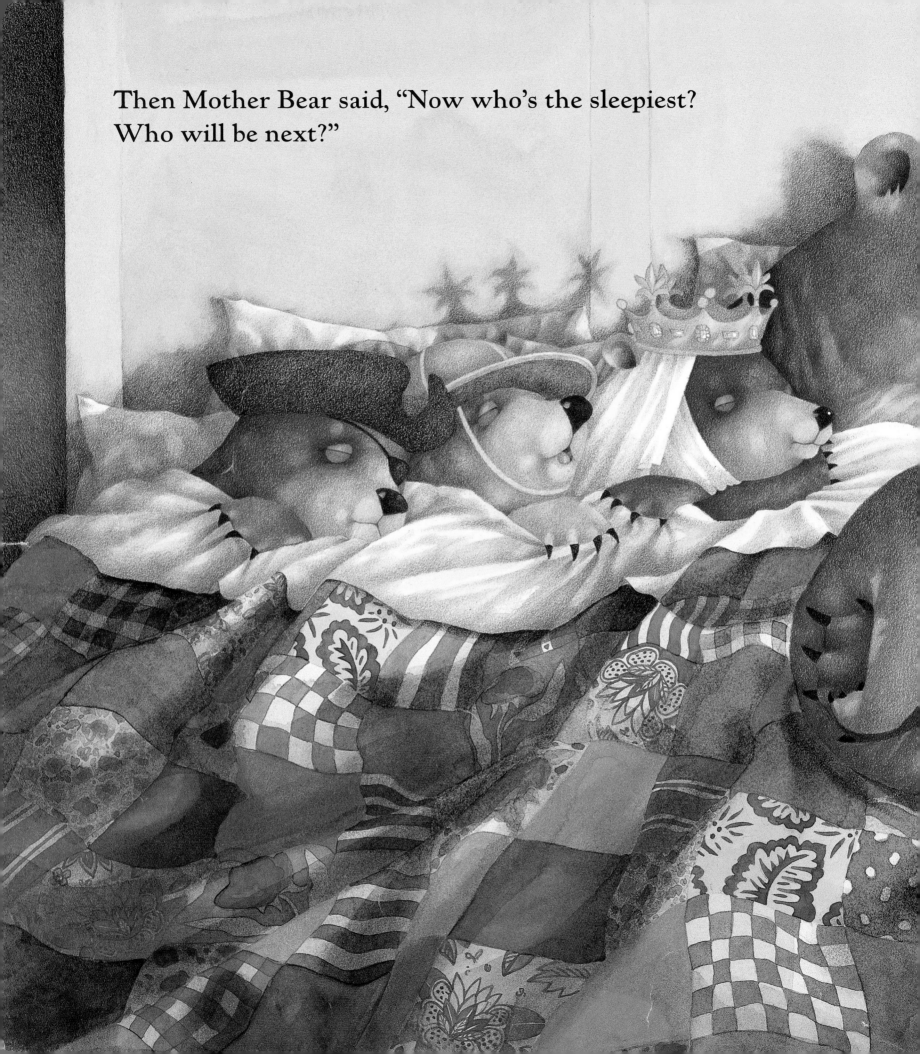

Ali Bear yawned a **BIG** yawn.

Mother Bear kissed his sleepy head and said,

"Ali Bear, Ali Bear,
Tummy all tight,
Dreaming of scrumptiousness
All through the night:
Chocolates and candy,
Sugar and spice,
Ices and syrups
And everything nice!"

And Ali Bear fell *faaaast* asleep.

Then Baby Bear yawned a BIG yawn.

Mother Bear smiled and said, "I know who's the sleepiest! I know who's next!"

She kissed his sleepy head and said,

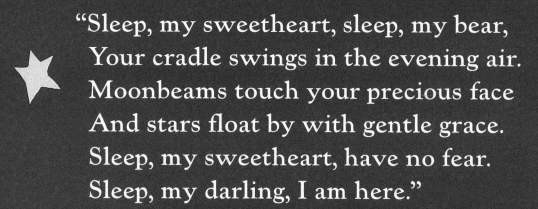

"Sleep, my sweetheart, sleep, my bear,
Your cradle swings in the evening air.
Moonbeams touch your precious face
And stars float by with gentle grace.
Sleep, my sweetheart, have no fear.
Sleep, my darling, I am here."

Then guess what happened?

Both Baby Bear *and* Mother Bear fell *faaaast* asleep in their soft feather bed.